Max's Christmas

ROSEMARY WELLS

Dial Books for Young Readers

NEW YORK

For Beezoo Wells

Published by Dial Books for Young Readers
375 Hudson Street
New York, New York 10014

Printed in Hong Kong by South China Printing Co.
Designed by Atha Tehon
C O B E
10
Library of Congress Cataloging-in-Publication Data
Wells, Rosemary, Max's Christmas.
Summary: Max waits up on Christmas Eve to see
Santa Claus coming down the chimney.
[1. Christmas — Fiction. 2. Santa Claus — Fiction.
3. Rabbits — Fiction.] I. Title,
PZ7.W46843Masg   1986   [E]   85-27547
ISBN 0-8037-0289-2
ISBN 0-8037-0290-6 (lib. bdg.)

The full-color artwork consists of black line-drawings and
full-color washes. The black line is prepared and
photographed separately for greater sharpness and contrast.
The full-color washes are prepared with colored inks.
They are then camera-separated and reproduced as
red, yellow, blue, and black halftones.

Guess what, Max!
said Max's sister Ruby.
What? said Max.

It's Christmas Eve, Max, said Ruby,
and you know who's coming!
Who? said Max.

Santa Claus is coming,
that's who, said Ruby.
When? said Max.

Tonight, Max, he's coming tonight!
said Ruby.
Where? said Max.
Spit, Max, said Ruby.

Santa Claus is coming right down
our chimney into our living room,
said Ruby.
How? said Max.

That's enough questions, Max.

You have to go to sleep fast,
before Santa Claus comes, said Ruby.

But Max wanted to stay up
to see Santa Claus.
No, Max, said Ruby.

Nobody ever sees Santa Claus.
Why? said Max.
BECAUSE! said Ruby.

But Max didn't believe a word
Ruby said.

So he sneaked downstairs...

and waited for Santa Claus.

Max waited a long time.

Suddenly, ZOOM! Santa
jumped down the chimney
into the living room.

Don't look, Max! said Santa Claus.
Why? said Max.
Because, said Santa Claus,
nobody is supposed to see me!

Why? said Max.
Because everyone is supposed to be asleep in bed, said Santa Claus.

But Max peeked at Santa anyway.
Guess what, Max! said Santa Claus.
What? said Max.

It's time for me to go away
and you to go to sleep,
said Santa Claus.
Why? said Max.

BECAUSE! said Santa Claus.

Ruby came downstairs.
What happened, Max? asked Ruby.
Who were you talking to?
Where did you get that hat?

Max! Why is your blanket
so humpy and bulgy?

BECAUSE! said Max.